Whispers from Below

Impressum:

Written by the T9A Team

Published by FlorianGressConsulting, Rosenweg 24, 93053 Regensburg, Germany

Printed by Amazon Media EU S.à r.l., 5 Rue Plaetis, L-2338, Luxembourg

ISBN: 978-3-9824212-6-1

THE IX AGE
FANTASY BATTLES

A 9TH AGE SUPPLEMENT

VERMIN SWARM
WHISPERS FROM BELOW

THE IX AGE
FANTASY BATTLES

A 9TH AGE SUPPLEMENT

VERMIN SWARM
WHISPERS FROM BELOW

Faction leader: Sebastiaan Follens

Head of Background: Edward Murdoch

Contributing authors: Sebastiaan Follens, Edward Murdoch,
Glenn Patel, John Wallis, Calisson, Ghiznuk

Editor: John Wallis

Layout: Kacper Bucki

First Edition 01/2022

Agatha,

I pray this package reaches you in time.
This is everything I could find. I hope it is enough.

They are on to me. My time is up. You MUST keep
these documents safe; you will know when to use them.

All I can say is I'm sorry I ever doubted you. You were
right from the start. The threat is real. Soon...they rise!

In Sunna's Light,
Luthor

HISTORY

The ancient Avrasi believed their city and greatness was founded by the twin brothers Avrulus and Evrulus, the orphans suckled by a she-wolf. The Vermin, who consider themselves the heirs of this legacy, believe it was not a lupine creature who nurtured the future heroes, but a rodent. Yes you may laugh, but the question of origins has proved a very serious one for many of us through the ages, both human and vermin. How, indeed, can we explain the events that ushered in the Age of Plague so many centuries ago? That is our topic for today.

There are a great number of theories about the Arrival, as we call the event that marked the end of the Fourth Age and brought the Swarm into the world. As you know, the Vermin were born during the siege of Avras, at the zenith of the Avrasi Civil War. The forces of the ambitious general Gaius Dexion fought those theoretically loyal to the Senate, led by the equally power-hungry Marcus Tiberian. More important to this tragic tale is the infamous priest-sorcerer and former statesman Quintus Augustus, who was languishing in a prison cell during the siege for daring to criticise the war and the conduct of Tiberian as general.

The popular telling has Augustus begging his people's Caelysian gods for salvation and an end to fighting in his dungeon cell. While the gods refused to answer, there was one who heard his prayers. The holy gem around the priest's neck suddenly became imbued with divine power, possibly by a supernal of the pantheon with mysterious intentions, supposedly granting Augustus the very "Fire of the Gods". The old man summoned the little dungeon rats to him, tying their tails together around the gem in an incantation of ancient design, creating a version of the "rat king" phenomenon known to occur naturally. It is suggested by some unlikely sources that this terrible creature, representing the birth of a verminous new species, would go on to become *The* Ratking: an enormous, evil ball of mad rats that supposedly still controls the Swarm in secret today, from the deep dark.

Regardless of such fanciful notions, the classical account continues. As Augustus' spell took effect, the rats began to grow – not just those he had tied together, but others nearby as well – swelling to human size, rising onto two feet, and overpowering the dungeon guards. The priest was carried from the jail to find the city gripped by fighting; Dexion had breached the walls and his legions fought Tiberian's in the streets. Only as vermin came forth in ever-growing numbers did the two sides pause.

Some say Augustus called for peace, others that he betrayed his creations and tried to smother them in the crib. In either case, both human armies were so horrified by what they saw that they joined forces in their final hour to destroy the rat-men. Yet it was for nought. They were soon overwhelmed, for the spell was still at the height of its power. For every human soldier devoured by rodents, new walking, thinking rats emerged, frenzied with fear, confusion and hunger, hardly understanding what they did as they consumed the city with terrible swiftness.

It is said that in later years, the Vermin developed their own myth of the Arrival. While the traditional story ends with Quintus Augustus fleeing, never to be heard from again, the Vermin account has him taken captive in the Senate House. A brave rat stepped forward, calling for mercy for their creator. Yet even as it spoke, it fell dying from a knife buried in its back by none other than the individual who would later call itself Gnaeus Primus Rodentius, the first rodent King of Avras, he who directed the Swarm so mercilessly to expand and consume the rest of the city's ancient territory across Vetia and beyond. In this account, Rodentius publicly used Augustus' innards for an augury, providing a sign that the gods had judged humanity no longer worthy of Avras' mantle, that the Vermin should now rule supreme – just as the gods slew and replaced their own parents, the titans.

Many have tried to explain how exactly Augustus or any other agent brought the Vermin into being. Divine intervention seems undeniable. Magic of this sort – that of true creation, not temporary conjuration or mere illusion – is beyond even the ken of the wisest elven sages from across the sea. Most Vermin sources point to Melkiope, the humble muse of tragedy, as the one who misled Quintus Augustus into bringing about the Arrival. Relegated from goddess to minor supernal by the Avrasi, she may have harboured foul resentment and dark ambitions. Among the Vermin she is venerated as the greatest of godheads, though she is considered a being to fear rather than love.

Some say that it was not the rats who grew large, but the entire population of the prison, guards and inmates alike, who were transformed into ratmen. Such an idea bolsters the Vermin's insistence that they are the true heirs of Avras, being, in effect, simply the descendants of humans who were placed under a permanent curse.

A more outlandish theory claims that the ratmen are not of this world at all, and crossed over from another place beyond the Veil, perhaps sent as a punishment for the moral decay of the Avrasi Empire, or via dark sorcery initiated by the agents of Chaos or Undeath. In this version of the tale, popular among the clergy of the Church of Sunna, the Vermin are the personification of mankind's sins, intended to castigate us for our transgressions. Alas, there is no evidence for any such claims.

It is believed that use of the term "Arrival" to describe the event began immediately after Avras fell to the Vermin. Modern archaeological and chronomantic research has confirmed that at least some of the ratmen were literate from the very start. They produced a surprising number of primary sources on their early history as they sought to make sense of their coming into the world. Initially written in classical Avrasi but later devolving into a bastardised version of that tongue, it seems that Vermin scholars have long been as interested and divided on the topic as we are today.

Tomorrow we shall provide an overview of Vermin history between the Arrival and the Goddess, including the ten thousand children of Gnaeus Primus, attempts at legal codification, the Warborn and pre-Infernal wars, arcane experimentation in the Ruined Quarter, and the rat-witch Sycorax who became the first Dictator.

—From the lectures of Mundhir al-Musa, Dawnlight Chair of History at the University of Avras

Avras has fallen. The ratmen came from within the walls and beneath our feet, overrunning the greatest city in the world in less than a day. We managed to escape in the chaos, to regroup and plan our next move from a safe haven in the interior province of Glauca. We are a sorry crew, poorly equipped, cut off from aid. The Vermin have devoured our grain and plundered our heirlooms with only slightly less zeal than they showed in consuming our very bodies. They roam the city at will, burning, murdering and enslaving the good souls who could not flee. Had we not been undone by jealousy and fear of our own people, we might have repulsed them.

Dexion's treachery has ruined us. With his pale queen pouring honeyed words in his ear, he would have ushered in an era of death and tyranny. Some say he was slain in the fighting, others whisper that his mistress has given him a gift that transcends death… Still, Avras has paid the price for their ambition.

All we can do now is wait. Our legions have proven themselves capable of defeating a more numerous foe time and time again. We shall regroup and let the Swarm starve itself in winter. Come the spring, we shall purge the ratmen from our glorious city and restore the Republic.

Avras remains lost to us. Patrician families fight among themselves, seeming content to let the ratmen squat in its ruins for months now – or perhaps they fear to disturb the nest.

Yet I worry something dark stirs in the ruins of Avras. I have seen Vermin scouting parties roaming as far as Myra, clad in the garb of legionaries and clumsily wielding looted weapons and shields. It seems they even speak our tongue, albeit in their own chittering fashion. A most curious sight, but it bodes ill for the future. Perhaps they are not the savage beasts we thought them to be?

Every spring, they come. Vermin legions striking out from Avras, disorganised at first, but learning with every battle. They send envoys ahead of their legions bearing decrees from their king, who is called Gnaeus Primus Rodentius, demanding our surrender and reintegration into his empire. It is said he holds court in the ruins of the Senate House, attended by a chamber of screeching vermin in filthy togas.

We laughed and routed the Vermin rabble those first years, but it seems they are without number. Rodentius' stratagems have grown more cunning, and every year his armies grow larger and bolder. Like the tides, they flood and ebb, testing us, wearing us down. His legions march out into the provinces, consuming all in their path, seeking to feed their unending hunger and forge an empire of their own. Laughter has turned to bitter silence and fear.

I fear that our strength may soon be too little to stop him, so I have invoked the old alliance our people held with the dwarves. Since their declaration of neutrality at the outset of the civil war, they have begun to fortify their mines and cities even more elaborately, but they must recognise the Vermin will one day threaten us all. We must stand together as we once did, allies in iron.

It is over. Our legions are shattered, and the dwarven Emperor is gravely wounded. The dwarves have retreated back to the mountains, and will not answer our hails.

How did it come to this? For years, we fought so hard to prevent the rise of a tyrant, and the Republic was torn apart because of it. Now, a king rules in Avras all the same.

The old families have laid down their arms and pay tribute to a Vermin oppressor in food and hostages. The shame is too much to bear.

I wonder if the gods mock us, sending these rodents to punish us for our hubris and ambition. It matters little, for our priests and oracles can no longer find any answers. The gods have fallen silent, and I wonder if they have turned their backs on us for our sins.

So ends the fourth age of this world. Our sun has set, and the time of the Swarm has come.

—Papyrus fragments dating from approximately 820-794 B.S.

LEGACY

I was woken one morning by a sound I had not heard in years: hooves. In my nightshirt, I went to the door, from which I can see almost the whole island. A boat had docked at the jetty and four armoured horsemen were approaching. Equitans. From the lead horse sprang a young woman.

"They tell me that you know all there is to know about the rats who walk like men," she said.

"Is that what they say?" I smiled. "Last I heard, my testimony was deemed nothing but malicious and heretical fairy tales, by decree of the Supreme Prelate."

"I serve the Lady of Cups, not the Supreme Prelate, and I would hear these tales," said the woman. I did not wonder at her manner; I had guessed she was royalty. We went inside and I made a fire to heat soup. The knights stood stiffly just outside the door.

"I should warn you that I cannot tell you many certain truths about the Vermin," I began. "We still know so little. But there is one fact of which I am sure. They have built a second Avras."

The eyes of the princess gleamed from behind the steam rising from her bowl of broth. I continued:

"I know the notion is hard to credit. But if you wish to understand the Vermin, you must return to the beginning. You must put yourself into the mind of a species that emerged fresh and terrified into the world like a newborn babe. Its only parent, the city where it spawned, was devoured in its early madness. Those first vermin, multiplying so rapidly, were left utterly alone, without direction or instruction, abandoned in the wilderness like the founding twins of Avras itself.

"Only one certain belief saved them from ruin in those first days: that they had been called forth by destiny. Their creation they saw as a divine signal of their calling: they were the true heirs of civilisation. From the very beginning, the Vermin became obsessed with the empire they had inherited, hunting for the records and history of its people. Like many of us, they both loved and hated their parent, despising its failures, grieving its demise, yearning for its approval, and most of all, desperate to prove that they, the Vermin, were a worthy and indeed superior successor. Everything they do, they do in emulation of the ancients. It is the very cornerstone of their identity, purpose and culture.

"The Swarm worships many of the same Caelysian gods, is ruled by the same forms of government, and organises its armies by the same principles found in human Avras of antiquity. Its legions march under the same eagles, and we even see the same military strategies on the field. Do you doubt that they would seek to rebuild the same city?"

"It's a fascinating thought, but don't you think we would know if there was a second copy of the largest city in the world?" asked the maiden.

"Perhaps, or perhaps not, your Highness. There are many places in this world we do not go." I pointed at the floor. "Why do you think I live on this tiny rock in the middle of the ocean? It is the only place I do not fear what lies beneath – and sometimes I think even that is a foolish faith.

"The Vermin seek to copy their predecessors, but they are rarely skilled in doing so. Their vision of Avras is like a corpse raised by a necromancer, an uncanny semblance, but ultimately a mockery, a twisted parody of the true living soul. The gods which remained kept their names, but their natures changed grotesquely. Their government codifies the same systems, makes use of the same symbols, but its principles and methods would be unconscionable to a true Avrasi. Slaves, once an orderly and limited way to dispose of conquered enemies, are taken from their own people, outnumbering free vermin. And their swarming legions would not be recognisable to any who had witnessed the disciplined might of the first, human empire. Even the mighty eagle, symbol of inviolate Avrasi dominion, has been used so over-enthusiastically that it no longer represents a single legion, and is often carried by individual regiments.

"The second Avras is the same: a twisted mirror of humankind, an inversion, created in secret and in darkness, where the light of the gods never reaches. It lurks and festers there, ever dreaming of reclaiming its place in the sun. I think it was directly beneath the human city itself, though I was in the dark so long, I cannot be sure."

"You mean to tell me you have seen this place, with your own eyes," asked the Princess, and she leaned forwards, her gaze piercing.

"I have, your Highness. With my own eyes."

—The journal of Adriana of Jurado, Destrian theologian and archaeologist

2/2

POLITICS

Gather round for your lesson, my lovely pups. If you ever wish to be more than pipsqueaks, you must understand the system you live in. We call it the Game of Life and Death, or "democracy".

It all began after the Sun Witch came and drove us below the ground, killing our last Rex. That was a time of terrible woe. We, the people chosen by the gods, were reduced to a squeaking and humiliated frenzy. In our terror we turned on each other, and died in our thousands from starvation and civil war.

We were saved by brave priests who reminded us of the ancient Avrasi tradition of voting. And so we began the system that endures to this day: the people choose those who rule them, electing the many tribunes and the four consuls, our highest office, each consul able to veto the others. They rule with the support and guidance of the eternal Senate, a body appointed according to wealth and prestige.

The Senate was at its most powerful in those first days; we all turned to the glowing purple stripes of the senatorial togas to show us our new life in the dark. But politics moves quickly, my friends, and many regimes have risen and fallen over the long years. Some have tried to usurp the Senate and claim full power for themselves, becoming Rex in all but name. Sometimes one of the Great Houses has amassed so much influence that it effectively controls the entire government. There have been glorious revolutions aplenty, Dictators who think themselves gods, great speeches and show trials, even theocracies led by one priesthood or another. I still remember the slave revolts, and the military coup that followed when I was just a pup.

Each chapter of our history changes us, adding something new to the tapestry of our great destiny as a people. Your forefathers would not recognise our elections today; they would not even recognise our language, which has evolved to the point that only educated rodents know how to speak the classical tongue of our ancestors.

What we have today is a great complexity of systems added atop each other. We have the Houses, where you can seek patronage and education, if you can show loyalty or aptitude. We have the many temples of the gods, allegiances changing as often as their divine patrons in the myths. We all belong to one of the broad families – a gens, or *jent*, as you would say – these can be patrician or plebeian or both, and some wield great influence.

We all know the looming power of the legions and the city guard, and the elite praetorians who are known to play kingmaker. But even more than this, every senator fears the mob most of all. For when we are united as a swarm, we are unstoppable. And the mob may be easily distracted by games and triumphs, but the mob is always hungry. If you want to rule, you have to feed us, and we'll eat anything. Crops if we can grow them – grain above, but more likely fungus or sea-scum below. Hunting, fishing, shellfish diving, giant-insect farming, scavenging the stores and refuse of surface-dwellers, and anything we can get by trading with those who will meet us. One way or another, you need full bellies if you're going to get anywhere.

Today, we see three main political factions in Avras, and you must choose your allegiance wisely.

First come the Long Whiskers, a faction founded by the late Felix Aries, who led the uprising against the Praetoriat, forty years ago. Their leaders are the wealthiest and fattest landlords and usurers in Avras, with the support of many client families. They claim to be the proponents of tradition, morality and decency, and control many temples and scholars, as well as several leading figures among the Houses.

Second are the Gratchists. These are mostly small traders, clerks, industry workers and House-rats. Plebs. They are jealous of the Whiskers' wealth, and despise their use of slave labour, calling for more work for citizens. They present themselves as patriots, often filling the ranks of the legions with their supporters. Their founder, Ronchit of *jent* Babulia, used the teachings of the ancient human Gratchi brothers, calling for democratic reforms to ensure every true Avrasi gets a vote – he succeeded in reinstating the tribunes, but currently he languishes in a cell. Still, the Gratchists rule over several districts in the City, maintaining order with their vigilantes, violently attacking meetings organized by the other factions.

Finally there are the Free Rats. Those scorned for their dubious origins. The "jentless". Slaves and former slaves. Self-made rats. The Diseased. Many of our parents and grandparents came to Avras from the provinces looking for food, work and protection, gaining the trust of the higher society, rising to important administrative offices. Led by Onjet Vatchrem, they control whole sectors of the State apparatus, growing in wealth and clever alliances. All scorn the Free Rats, but all need them too.

So how can you carve your own career, my naive ones? First you must make a living. Find a generous sponsor, who listens to his clients and heeds their petitions. Avoid those who will have you pass through armies of clerks before ever reaching their ears: you need someone who will not be ashamed to receive you in person in his apartments. Protection, however, will always be in proportion to your loyalty. You need to show a true dedication to your master and political family. They need to see that the resources they spend on you are well spent, indeed, that they serve to increase their personal influence and fame.

Flatter your superiors and talk up your own achievements. Show that you bring supporters to them, but do not give the impression that you seek supporters for yourself, or they will destroy you. Bide your time, and soon your paunch will start getting rounder and rounder. Know when to strike at your competitors who stand on the same rung as you, but also know when to let them fight each other.

Seek new friends, and never make enemies unless you can eliminate them. Remove your rivals from any living tunnels under your supervision. During elections, mobilise as many as you can to your side of the line, and ensure they remain there until the end of the tail-count, lest they be dragged or scared away by rivals. Make sure your enforcers are reliable – you will need intelligence as well as strength.

Eventually, you may seek higher offices. If you are with the Whiskers you will most easily become one of the quaestors or pontifices. The Gratchists will make you a tribune, either domestic or military. The Free Rats will appoint you a major supervisor or help you create your own business. Finally, you may find a place as a senator, if you are popular with your peers, or as a consul, if you are popular with the mob.

With direct access to the State's feeding trough, your clients will now number in the hundreds. Be a good master, receive your clients in the same way that you wanted to be received when you were young, while never forgetting to show off your personal girth, wealth and prestige, to attract more clients. Listen much, talk little. Don't forget to forge private ties with other factions: you may be opponents today, but you could easily become allies tomorrow. Cultivate your own network within the Houses, the temples and the legions. And don't rise too fast or get too greedy, or you will find that Dusk will fall.

—Recorded words of Vrotch Trit Chichira to his youngest clients

2/2

FOOD

Once upon a time, in the small, quaint town of Hammerlin, lived the happiest people of the Empire, under the wise leadership of Mayor Cornelius. Cows were fat, granaries were full, fruits clumped on the trees in orchards, and hops overflowed from barrels.

It was a warm day of summer, when suddenly all the peasants ran from their fields and fled to the safety of the city: a troop of ratmen was approaching!

The mayor ordered the guard to man the walls and to ring the bells. To everyone's surprise, the tolling seemed to fill the ratmen with joy, and they came forward, greeting the Hammerlinners with cheers.

The rats were few in number and they looked thin and weak. One of the ratmen spoke Avrasi, with a strange accent. His name was Kronlit Hairyclaw. He explained that they were hungry but had gold to pay for food. If Hammerlin would sell to them, more gold would come.

The population was divided, but finally the promise of gold convinced them to accept the deal. Wilfried, the town prelate, predicted that a cataclysm would fall upon the people, but nobody listened to the warning.

So the ratmen built their own town, Ratterlin, just beyond the hill, or rather, under it. With the truce in effect, the ratmen asked regularly for food, and paid with gold. Many wondered where this gold was acquired, but none dared to speak the question aloud.

A year passed. Time had come for the traditional beer festival, the Tandemarfest. Kronlit Hairyclaw heard about the festivities, and sure enough, when the Ratterlinners came for food again, they also wanted to buy musical instruments and pompous street bunting. The Hammerlinners were happy to oblige.

Then the ratmen's attitude changed.

The next time the Hammerlinners saw Kronlit, he wore luxurious clothes and had an escort.

He explained that the feast and the food pleased the ratmen, and they were now calling him Maskin Heroclaw, which meant something like the biggest. He was now the Mayor of Ratterlin.

He started to ask for more. The townsfolk were only too pleased to gain more gold for the food they thought was worth so little. But the more food the Hammerlinners provided, the more the Ratterlinners asked, and the more the rodent population seemed to grow. Their mayor also wanted more festivities: racing chariots, wrestling ring fences, banquet tables, fancy tablecloths, drums and bells. Bread and circuses – the needs of the ratmen seemed never to be fully satisfied.

Finally, there came a time when the rats were so numerous that the peasants became afraid again and took refuge in the town. The farms were left undefended and were pillaged. No grain, no cattle remained after the visit of the ratmen, only golden coins left behind. Soon the ratmen ate all the crops before they were ripe. They swarmed the lands, consuming even leather, straw, wood and manure. Nothing was left to eat in the whole region.

The population of Hammerlin was starving inside their walls. They had enough gold to plate their bowls but nothing to put inside. There were too many ratmen in the country for the guards, and no messenger could be sent out to call for help.

It was a gloomy winter day when a musician arrived in town. He was dressed in pied clothes like some followers of the Equitan trickster god, and played a sweet melody on his pipe. He went to meet Mayor Cornelius, claiming that he could get rid of the ratmen. The Mayor promised more than a king's ransom if he could repel the swarm of rats.

1/2

The pied piper walked towards the hill, playing tunes similar to those of the Tandemarfest. All the rat-men followed him behind the hill of Ratterlin.

One week later, the pied piper came back. He was carrying in a bag the head of Maskin Kronlit. He asked for his reward.

But now that the threat was gone, the city council was reluctant to oblige. Wilfried the prelate explained with a sententious tone that the death of the ratmen had nothing to do with the piper. It had sufficed for Hammerlin to stop feeding them. The rats who did not die from starvation killed each other, start-ing with their incompetent mayor. He added that vermin society always works like that, growing and shrinking with the food available, acclaiming or despising their leaders accordingly. He concluded that therefore, no reward was due.

The musician smiled darkly. "That may be. But a reward I was promised, a reward I shall take," he said. As they laughed him out of the council, he calmly took his pipe and started to play a melody. Once again, it sounded like feasts, abundant meals and playful games. All the town's children gathered around him, craving food and fun. And the pied piper left the town, followed by the children, in the direction of Rat-terlin.

The children were never seen again, and neither were the ratmen, but unusual numbers of ordinary rats plagued the townsfolk in the years that followed – all fat and with a wicked gleam in their eyes. Many years have passed, and still, in dark winters, the Hammerlinners can sometimes hear a nostalgic pipe melody from behind the hill.

Moral: Children, never trust a stranger (or a politician) dressed in fancy clothes and promising food and games. And always pay the piper!

—"The Pied Piper of Hammerlin", from Tales for Children, by the Brothers Gorry

GREAT HOUSES

So your lordship wants to know about the whiskered squeakers, eh? Not my place to ask questions, hur hur. Would be my genuine pleasure to tell a civilised gentleman like yourself all about the dark and scary underworld what you posh fellahs have never even dreamed of.

First thing you have to know: they's organised. You probably think about rats like you think about the rest of us: big stupid mob of dirty plebs. And you'd be right – they's no different to us. We've got the gangs what run the city, they've got something they like to call Houses. Like guilds, maybe, if the guilds were armed to the teeth and had their hands in the Emperor's money bag. They's got at least a dozen of em, but there's only a handful you really need to know about.

You'll no doubt be familiar with House Sicarra – if not, then you ain't been in this line of work very long, have you? Masterful thieves and smugglers, they are. Got a network of nastiness all across the civilised lands. Sometimes late at night you can even spot them in the shadows in lowtown – right here on the streets of Sunna's own Empire. They's almost as bad as the taxman, showing up wherever they's not wanted, taking their cut from our hard-earned ill-gotten gains. Still, they's better than tariffs and customs, that's why us honest traders still deal with em. You'd better watch yer back, of course – they'll double cross yeh as soon as sneeze at yeh. But don't even think of doing the same to them. Their memories are long, and their daggers longer.

Now I've never been in a vermin hole, but from what I hear, they's big. They've got whole cities down there, in some places, and where you got a mob of rats, you need something to keep em happy. My whiskered contacts, all they want to talk about most of the time is the games – arena fights to be specific. And what kind of beasties are fightin' in those deep-dark arenas? The ones made by House Fetthis. These rats are beast keepers and trainers, they breed all kinds of ghastly monsters, from those dire rats as big as hounds to their dim-witted, hulking brutes. They know their monsters like an Equitan knows his horses. Some of em's in the slave trade too, I hear – but I stay clear of that. The way they look at us humans gives me the shivers, to be honest. It's like they's considering how long we'd survive in a fighting pit with one of their brutes, or what price we'd fetch if they could sell us to the Qassari salt mines.

Those fancy guns you've no doubt seen in vermin paws? Made by the crazy buggers of House Rakachit. For your sake, I hope you've never been on the receiving end like I have. Despite being as mad as a bag of rats, as it were, they's a cunning bunch, good for business. Spend all their time dreaming up wild new inventions and mechanisms, but at least they understand supply and demand. Always ready to reach a deal. They's eager to buy darkstone and will pay a pretty pfennig to take those black crystals off your hands. I never understood why they want it so badly – the dwarven jewellers on the Sunnastrasse won't touch the stuff. I reckon the rats have a whole different line of craftlore. Some of em carry contraptions that might seem magical – ominous humming, arcing lightning making their fur stand on end. But my good friend at the university told me there's no real magic involved, not really. Whatever the case may be, stand well back from a Rakachit mouse if you're wearing too much metal.

Half the bedtime stories you've heard about the villainous ratmen are based on House Skorchit, and most of em's true as well. They consort with beings of the nether realms, stir large cauldrons of brews and potions, abduct imperial children from their beds, curdle the cow's milk – the works. It's a small House, but no less dangerous than the others. Fancy magic lore, alchemy, the Realm Beyond – all things that would land an honest man on a witch hunter's pyre, but they don't fear the fire, oh no. "Per ignem gloriam perveniamus" – that's what I heard one scream before he immolated himself with a malfunctioning flamethrower: "Glory through fire". That accursed Deepfire – that's their handiwork. Nearly impossible to put out, and it burns far longer than it should. The dreaded toxic mist, what makes soldiers spew their lungs? Also theirs, damn their eyes. I've even heard rumours that Skorchit is to blame for the Ruined Quarter of Avras – they tried to bargain with the Dark Gods in ages past, and the city paid the price for it.

Last one I should mention, though you'll almost never see em in these parts – I mean here near the surface. House Stygia. Their domain is the Deeps, ruling over places considered far down even by the bearded folk. They say some of em never even come as "high" as the vermin burrows themselves. They're miners mostly, content to stay in their underworld realm searching for ores, gems and new passageways. No one has a clue how far the true Deeps run, not dwarves or rats or goblins – but these Stygians are always tryin' to find out and delve deeper. On the rare occasions when they do decide to pay the surface world a visit, you can't miss them. They use these gigantic drills, louder than my mam when she's wanting tea, making the whole ground shake. I hope you never have to see a sinkhole like the one I saw in Narrenwald when I was new in this gig. Entire village swallowed by the earth. Course, the Dark Gods got the blame, thanks to our obliging Inquisition – something about the impious townsfolk bringing it on themselves, as per bloody usual.

All this talk of vermin has gotten me hungry for some cheese. Fetch some from the pantry, won't you? And bring a bottle of Entragues red to wash it down with!

—Words of former imperial operative and notorious smuggler Herrig Schwindelmeister,
a wanted man in three provinces and occasional consultant to the Imperial Spymasters

SLAVERY

SLAVES! THE CITY NEEDS YOU!

Is your owner treating you badly?

Don't die as a slave.

JOIN THE ARMY!

Break free from the debt trap!

In Senator Ajutch's legion,

twenty years of servitude become

twenty months of service.

Run and escape your owner!

You don't need their permission

to join the military!

Your past crimes and debts will be forgotten.

Fight for a worthy cause, for Avras!

Forget the whip, drop the chains.

Live the whisker-to-whisker camaraderie.

Eat robust legionary meals every day!

Fight and survive,

you may be promoted.

Become an infantry legionary

and you will vote as a citizen!

Join up at an Ajutch legion recruiting station

TODAY!

Bring fellow slaves who can't read

and you will get extra rations.

—Pamphlet found on half the corpses of 250 poorly equipped vermin soldiers

FREEDOM AND TYRANNY

I have always preached that there is great virtue in submission. Of course, my meaning was in particular relation to the Goddess Above, but many have used my words in reference to Aschau or Reva, and I have never objected. Still, ever since I left the pulpit to pursue my research into the mortal life of Her Holiness, I have found myself thinking more and more about submission.

At first, my intention was to know more about the last King of the rats in Avras, that great villain of scripture, second in infamy only to the Sunslayer, who had filled its flesh with so much power that it could stand against the Goddess Herself. Her commanders all swore that at its first appearance it had seemed no more than a normal-sized vermin.

As you know, I discovered at the Temple of Petrakos ancient papyri bearing the lost testimony of Natassa, a renowned lieutenant of Arcaleone, who had been captured prior to the reclamation of Avras, and had endured long months of imprisonment before her liberation by Sunna's forces. She swore that she witnessed the foul machinery and sorcerous rituals the King used to join itself with some grim avatar of the twisted vermin gods. Thus empowered, its ruthless authority multiplied, driving the city's defenders to battle despite their great terror of Sunna's wrath. By its own subjects it was no longer called *rex* but *dictator*, the special rank reserved by the ancient Avrasi for those granted extraordinary powers for a limited period in order to overcome outstanding threats to the city.

I diligently compared Natassa's account to that of others who have survived the captivity of the Swarm. On most points they aligned: the Dictator was a creature dreaded by vermin of all classes. It appears that – like all parts of the rodents' classical heritage – this figure became a nightmarish perversion of its original conception. Where the dictator was a hero to the ancients, a public servant of exceptional humility and honour, willing to give up power after danger was averted, to the rats it was a hated oppressor and a tyrant. Even the most ambitious senators shuddered at the prospect, for in merging with a supernal, the rat would forfeit part of its very identity and often its sanity.

Yet when a grave enough peril was faced, or when a vermin leader became sufficiently desperate or vainglorious, the ritual would be attempted. We know of several such moments over the centuries. It requires unpredictable technologies and enormous energy (both mundane and magical), but it has proven successful on enough occasions to have left a lasting legacy in the Vermin psyche. Sometimes, a Dictator's titanic power succeeded in overcoming the threat that was faced, but this was cold comfort, for the victorious creature would swiftly become more tyrannical than ever, inflicting misery after misery on its people.

Through this research, I had discovered a people in thrall to the most despotic of rulers. A nation of craven underlings, a species that reeked of submission, surely. And yet the more I learned, the muddier this picture became. Dictators were clearly the exception to the rule. Most of Vermin history was free of their touch, and indeed many steps had been taken to prevent their coming or to end the reign of those that did arise.

Vermin interrogated in captivity universally claim allegiance to the self-same symbols as the old Avrasi: SPQA, the Senate and the people of Avras (or sometimes SRQA, to appeal specifically to rodents). I remember the first time I heard this claim for myself, when I was permitted access to a subject captured in upper Glauca. He – or maybe she – snivelled that "Avras" had been a republic ever since Sunna slew the last rex. Despite their image of the Sun Maiden as a monstrous devil, many were secretly grateful to her for sparing them the reign of another Dictator. It appears that at least some vermin do truly value political freedom.

It is perhaps in mockery of the Dawn Goddess that we are told the Vermin call their ruling body the Senatus Vesperi, the Dusk Senate, and yet those were not the vermin captive's words. He was shocked at the implication, protesting that the Dusk Senate had no true authority, and that Avras was led, as it ever was, by the consuls and the Senate itself, an entirely separate and much more prestigious institution, its members considered upstanding citizens.

When I asked what, in that case, was the "Dusk Senate", the rodent grew quiet and replied only: *Senatus omnibus regnat*, sed tenebri. The Senate rules all but the dark.

I was forced to find the answer from (slightly) more salubrious sources: imperial soldiers. It seems that those who have met the Swarm in battle are sometimes cursed by an encounter with the Dusk Senate. According to those I met, "Dusk Senator" is what vermin call those warriors skilled in lethal violence, who seek to strike from the shadows and vanish again without trace. In short, the "Senatus Vesperi" is nothing but an association of assassins and cutthroats.

Perhaps we should not be surprised – and yet once again, the best and worst of the Swarm can often be found side by side. For these assassins are frequently mentioned in captured documents as a mysterious force not just to be feared, but also to be hoped for and relied upon. It appears that this shadowy institution has often been responsible for the fortuitous disappearance of a would-be autocrat or demagogue.

Perhaps this, then, is the ultimate duality of the Vermin. The sure antithesis of democracy – agents who murder elected officials with no oversight (aside from the theoretical threat of military reprisals) – and yet this very body is a champion of freedom, preserving the real Senate against threats both internal and external.

The whole business has given me cause to wonder if the Vermin are truly any different to us in their relationship to submission and defiance. For all their repulsiveness, they have thrown off their kings just as the Avrasi of old. It is true their hidden warrens are a nest of back-stabbers and rabble rousers, but then...I myself have spent time in Aschau. I find myself doubting if it is so different.

—*From the letters of Prelate Agatha Anthides, dated shortly before her excommunication*

GEOGRAPHY

November 14, 951 A.S.

I have returned to The City. Avras is fatter and shabbier than I remember. Many slovenly peoples and species mix freely under the sky. The stonework has decayed, the populace is engorged in numbers yet diminished in dignity, the pomp and circumstance have slowly ebbed away. Once, it ruled the world. Now, it doesn't even truly rule itself. Streets that once saw the triumphs of the greatest warlords of an age now only teem with merchants and beggars. It may be the largest city the world has ever known, but it has fallen far from the pedestal upon which my heart enshrined it.

November 23

Rumours of secret tunnels beneath the Grand Colosseum have taken my interest. When the Vermin were slaughtered in past ages, stories held that the survivors slunk away into dark tunnels. Perhaps some handful remain, and could be bent to Mother or even Grandmother's purposes.

November 33

My first incursion into the tunnels was less than optimal. Following the secret passages from the base of the Great Colosseum that my bats had uncovered, thralls were dispatched to conduct espionage. Only Rubio returned alive, and he barely. Still, his report was illuminating; the Vermin remain, and the tunnels lead to their domain.

Nundinum 2

More subtle reconnaissance proved a wise move; a hooded cloak, strong glamour and the diminutive stature of myself and some carefully chosen escorts fooled the vermin and allowed my passage into the depths below. Beholding the sights, my jaw went as slack as that of a provincial rube.

It was not merely the size, the scale, the grandeur. It was the mad chaos of the excess. Roads twice the width of those above, but zig-zagging madly across the cityscape when viewed from above. Monuments duplicated, triplicated and expanded with crazed architectural fantasies. Buildings too large to stand above the ground, held in place by the cavern walls. This was not a replica of Avras – this was a replica of a thousand maddened dreams of Avras, an idealization of the City illuminated eternally by flameless lamps.

Their Grand Colosseum sinks from the foundations of the one above, but spreads outwards – far more Colosseum lies beneath than above. One leaves the Colosseum, steps outside, makes progress... and finds a second Colosseum, this one dedicated to aquatic combat. Then a third, for racing instead of bloodshed, though one often accompanies the other. The spirit of the Games remains intact; the filthy hordes of man-shaped rats enjoy the public spectacles as much as the plebeians of Avras ever did. There are more of them than I ever dreamed – more than any of the surface world realises, mortal or immortal.

Once you learn to recognise them, all the great landmarks are there – including some that have since been lost to the city above. The great wheel once turned by the Omiphorus waterway now churns with the footfall of ten thousand paws, throwing sparks and lightning all around. And I would ascribe the Vermin some appreciation of the finer arts for their recreation of the Grand Theatre and the Imperial Palace, but their almost unintelligible screeching attempts at drama, and the artworks upon the walls of the Palace are copies of copies of copies; the original majesty long since distorted into hideous caricature.

They have rebuilt my city in the dark and soot. It sickens me almost as much as their taste in my mouth.

I must follow this thread further. How far does this mockery extend?

1/3

Ullos 29, 952 A.S.

I begin to grudgingly grant the Vermin some small consideration of their self-declared title as the "heirs of Avras". I have walked the spokes that stretch forth from Under-Avras, roads through caverns that lead in secret to the surface. The rats maintain the Imperial Highway on the surface, or at least they use long stretches of it, travelling after dark across the wilds of the Forsaken Marches – what was once the glory of Dannorica Prima, where Grandmother was Propraetor – to and from secret strongholds.

For they maintain many of the old colonies. I have seen maps of the rat's nest of paths spider-webbing out from Avras across the dangers of the surface world. Yet below the ruins of old Avrasi cities and fortresses, whose populations have died out and whose buildings have been left to crumble, the Vermin persist in hidden warrens. The ghost of the old empire endures.

Ullos 12, 953 A.S.

I have tested the limits of my glamour and wits. I have walked the Vermin Ways, I have followed their Senators (and in turn been followed by their death-dealing counterparts, I suspect), I have spoken with citizens of their Republic. I have enthralled dozens of rodents and ripped secrets from their minds as I took sustenance from their bodies. Their roads stretch further than ours ever did. They have cast off kings and emperors as once we did, a humbling contrast in this fallen age of monarchy. I still cannot claim to have found the length and breadth of the Vermin lands – a fact which, in itself, troubles me.

In the Copper Mountains, Messantium ("Mesnetch" in the vulgar tongue in common use today) has vanished from many human maps, but more trade flows through it now than even in the height of the Old Empire, smuggling fortunes in black market goods past dwarves, elves and Qassari.

The port of Daedalium is today known as Dajrin by the Vermin and Dados by the local Khasib population, who remain unaware that the caves around and below the harbour are home to parasitical and especially paranoid Avrasi rodents. These vermin are so afraid of discovery that they have protected their nest with endless traps and mazes – designs so complex that even their own number frequently forget the few safe ways to enter. Those of my own minions who survived reported sighting great rafts in secret caverns, made ready for emergency escapes.

Castra Nova, or Katchrenop, was likewise difficult to reach – the Crimson Peaks have long been treacherous to our Order, and nowadays there are the added threats of predatory beasts (both above and below the ground) and knightly expeditions to slay them. Though it lies beneath the ruins of a former regional capital, today it is a legionary staging ground ruled by a military council.

The mines of Nida were dwindling even in my day, but they are not exhausted, and the report I intercepted indicates the Vermin use it primarily as a base for espionage within Sohnstahl.

The "ghosts of Charazond" – well, I now know they do not serve any lodge of the Covenant. The old fortress, that the Vermin call Khrozed, is held by dusk-dwelling rats, who raid the steppe while attempting to remain hidden from vengeful horsemen and Warriors. The "ghost ships" are stolen vessels owned by Vermin slavers, reaping a crop of fear they did not rightly sow. This harvest crosses those blighted waters bound for the markets of Avras – both above and below, most likely.

While most colonies lie beneath the ruins of the ancients, there are a few notable exceptions. I was amazed to find reference to a city I'd never heard of, originally called Galba Maior but commonly known as Grevmoj – and when I finally reached it, even more amazed to discover that it rivals Under-Avras itself in size and grandeur, and almost in political importance. Founded by fleeing survivors at the start of this age, it is known for both inventiveness and rebelliousness. I was alarmed to encounter a large plague-worshipping population – but perhaps this could be an advantage should we need to incite conflict close to the capital.

Krendor (possibly a corruption of "Colonia Aurea" in good Avrasi) is another new colony – a literal goldmine expanded to the size of a small city, hidden in the forests of eastern Sonnstahl, built with the bizarre technologies of the Stygians and powered by the muscles of brutes and slaves.

Other ancient sites where I have confirmed a Vermin presence include Pityus (still an agricultural centre, according to reports – a rare and valuable thing to the vermin); Tarantium (the entire island fort is controlled by vermin, so they have no need to hide below ground); Taborenta (a holy city now held by the plague cult); and even Numentia on the borders of Sagarika – it was one of Old Avras' most distant cities, and it remains too distant for the Senate to fully control. This appears to be a rule for Vermin colonies: the longer it takes to reach them, the more independence they are able to claim. In fact, Numentia is currently under the thumb of the Dictator Cotemus, who has declared himself to be the incarnation of Iovanus and has begun to openly enslave nearby humans and vermin alike, using an army of horrors bred from local megafauna.

I am certain that there are even more distant colonies yet. Some claim wherever life can cling, their fellow vermin have gone. Silexia, Taphria, Augea, Virentia, mountains, jungles, frozen wastelands or molten mountains – I have heard these rumours and I believe many to be true. If I am indeed able to find such fables as the snow-vermin Ice Cities of the north, or even the warrens said to have emerged on the Western continents, I suspect that they will have little connection to Avras itself, having lost all contact with their progenitors and all memory of their heritage.

Whatever the case, I am certain that the schemes this information has already allowed me to put into motion will greatly expedite my rightful progress into the truest heart of the Covenant. My initiation as Master of the Ninth Talisman is all but assured.

—Sealed Archive. Recovered by the Inquisition from the abode of Claudia Quinta,
the master Lamian dubbed "the last Child of Avras"

GODS

Ever since we came into this world, we have been the faithful servants of the Caelysian gods. We are their children and they love and protect us as parents should, anointing us the true Avrasi. For long centuries our priests have tended their altars and observed their rites. Our rulers have always recognised their authority, and our temples have always served to guide the people and the princes alike.

But in recent times, many have fallen to worship of a heathen, foreign god, a monstrous creature of plague who comes from the East, who now has temples in the City itself. In their mad fervour, his diseased followers have forgotten their true heritage and their true gods. Their numbers spread and grow like the plague itself, leaving massed graves in their wake. Despite our best attempts at persecution, their influence has begun to reach onto the very floor of the Senate House.

It is imperative that we educate the common rodents in the nature and importance of the true gods. To that end I have created a simple guide to serve as an introduction. Know the gods, learn their names, and do not neglect your prayers, for they will remember your betrayal, and they will not forgive.

Mighty Melkiope, our great goddess of tragedy and prophecy, highest Queen, our first creator. She intervened to bring about the Arrival, hearing our prayers when no other would. The deceptive twists of fate and destiny are her design. Her chosen oracles perform augury for those seeking answers in the mists of the future and the past. But beware, for words of prophecy can often turn to tragedy.

Proud Iovanis, master of sky and the four winds, the lord of thunder and the soaring eagle. He longs for a forgotten age of Avrasi heroes, and scorns the prayers of the lowly even as he protects us from above. Only the mighty, the brave and the bold are worthy in his sight. He smites those who incur his wrath with holy lightning. His priesthood oversees the proper rituals for the Senate and the offices of the Republic.

Quiet Favana, the dark princess of the underworld, the mistress of magic. All the mineral wealth beneath the earth is hers, and comes to us through her magnanimity. Her greatest gift to us is darkstone, that sacred and divine crystal. She guards the souls of the dead beyond the last river, protected by her three-headed hounds. Her temples organise the funeral rites of the departed and guard the tombs of the Swarm against those who would defile them.

Vengeful Etris, the lady of the watery depths, mistress of the cold, briny seas and the dread tempest. All those who die drowning pass into her hellish underwater realm. Those who sail the waves would be wise to pay her homage, and pray for a swift return to dry land and warm burrows.

Cruel Acratos, armoured in blackest iron, the lord of the battlefield, master of war and conquest. In his name, our endless legions march across the world, tearing down the mighty and seizing their stores for plunder. His chosen march alongside the legions, inspiring the troops to greater ferocity in the warbringer's name.

Loving Vestaleia, the lady of hearth and home, the maiden of the sacred flame. Some say the ancients honoured her with their virginity, but we cannot believe any god would accept such an unnatural offering. Instead, we worship her hearth itself, and her priestesses tend her fires in their temples, observing the rituals necessary to preserve the everlasting greatness of our people.

Tireless Ateus, the grey-bearded lord of the forge, the master smith and artisan. The magnificent arms and armour of his siblings are crafted by his hand. His priests tend to the city's armouries and work among the great Houses.

Bright Nameus, the lord of healing, light and the arts. He is beloved among Caelysian believers, for his presence shields the Swarm from the horrors of plague, and he favours the sculptors, architects and musicians of the eternal city. Many of his shrines have been defaced of late, worshippers driven away by evil and pestilent infidels. But we will rebuild them!

Fierce Tarina, the Huntress, lady of woodlands and wild beasts, sister to Nameus. Keeper of the untamed places above our warrens and beyond the frontiers of explored surface areas. Ultimately, wild beasts both above and below the ground answer only to her, despite the best efforts of the beastmaster's whip and chain.

Jovial Udius, the master of feasts, lord of wine, discord and hunger. In his name we hold grand public banquets in the forums, where bread is plentiful and wine flows freely. Civil strife and chaos are his works, for he delights in the entertainment politics and war provide.

Patient Echo, elevated to godhood by those who took pity on her. Cursed by a jealous goddess to never speak again, she can only repeat what the gods themselves say unto her. Under the tutelage of Ateus and Nameus, she forged the great bells to guide us in the dark. But beneath their ominous tolling, one can hear her servants whisper in the shadows, seeking to further her unfathomable goals.

Grim Sastus, the hidden master of doorways, shadows and sudden change, the protector of the Republic. He is the hidden lord of the Dusk Senate and its feared cadre of assassins who are ever-watchful to prevent the rise of a tyrant who, in his hubris, would lead the Republic to ruin.

There are many Forgotten Ones too, gods worshipped by the humans of Avras that are now lost to the mists of history. These are the gods who turned their backs against us when we were born, rejecting the worship of the new generation, the heirs of their own legacy. Preferring to fade into ignominious obscurity, their temples and statues were left to crumble, and their absence remains a scar in the Swarm's spiritual consciousness – though we have proved our worth without their aid.

We have forgotten the name of the goddess of peace and love, the goddess of wisdom, the goddess of the harvest, and the god of messages. They do not answer our prayers. We do not know how many others may have been lost as well.

There is one other we have not forgotten. The wretched Sol, the great Enemy, she whose look is burning fire, whose touch is boiling agony. Once we believed she protected us as she did Avras of old. But we have learned her scorching lessons, and we will not trust the Sun's light again.

—Passages from a book carried by a vermin priest captured by Volskayan outriders

THE PLAGUE CULT

Far to the east, in Sagarika, the land of a thousand gods,

Men and Vermin lived side by side in peace.

In a time wracked by plague, a ratchild was born.

He who would become the Shepherd.

He who endured when all others succumbed.

The lone ratchild grew and became wise.

He travelled the land and spoke to the brahmins.

But their words rang hollow.

He undertook a voyage to Mount Faoshan

To speak with the gods and seek the truth of the world.

For forty days he fasted and meditated at Bodh Goru.

The many deities of Sagarika and beyond appeared before him.

A thousand gods, a thousand lies;

The Shepherd despaired at their deceit and duplicity.

Then came Errahman the all-embracing, the Plaguebringer.

He showed him the truth of life in this World.

All that lives must die: all will wither and decay.

Plague and death are not things to be feared or shunned.

They are the fate of all beings.

This world is a crucible of sin and corruption.

Suffering brings salvation;

Those who are marked by plague are blessed,

And will know peace in the hereafter.

Errahman blessed the Shepherd and named him Barbas, the Prophet

Commanding him to begin the great work.

He travelled across lands of ash and flame
Fire-marked dwarves beholden to wicked gods assailed him.
Barbas brought plagues down upon them and freed their vermin slaves,
Teaching them the truth of the world.
He led his people through the Sea of Thirst.

The Shepherd went west to rejoin the first Swarm.
They had lost their way and paid homage to many vain gods.
Their empire had crumbled before the might of sun and steel;
Barbas would show them the true path.
The Senate feared him.
With daggers in the dark, they slew him at Taborenta.
But they could not stop the word of Errahman.

The faith grew strong despite its persecution.
The poor, the burdened and the shackled found solace and brotherhood.
Plague will spread, bringing glory upon the world.
The righteous shall accept their baptism, like the Shepherd before.
And through plague, we shall find salvation.
So it is written, so shall it be.

—Litany of Eshkael Contanimus Venerabilis, disciple of Prophet Barbas

TECHNOLOGY

Honourable Guild Masters,

I have returned after twenty years. I was taken prisoner by the rodents. I was forced into bondage to Vermin engineers. I held true to my oaths. I shared no secret of guild or craft. My roots remain in the Deep.

I return with what I have learned.

Some have called "Vermin technology" a contradiction in terms. They are wrong. It is real, and it is a threat. As you'd expect from a people with no honour, Vermin engineers do everything the opposite of the right way. They experiment rather than hold to tradition. They accept failure, repeatedly, as if it were a fact of life. In their perversity, these methods produce results – albeit at the cost of many wasted resources and lives.

I thought for years that the shaky foundations of Vermin technology were certain to collapse into senseless confusion. Yet there is progress in their madness. Within the great guilds of their city, which they call Houses, they search ceaselessly for new inventions. Each House distinguishes itself from the others by unique processes and techniques, all competing against each other or occasionally entering into brief and uneasy alliances. Yet no master teaches any apprentice. No tomes or records are kept for future guild members. Instead, they often disguise their work or leave hazardous decoys, wary of the spies of other Houses. To my amazement, when these false experiments are recreated, pure serendipity can even lead to actual discoveries. This is how they advance.

Vermin mine not only sacred metals and stones. They also have uses for many wasteful ores, such as favanite, favored by their sorcerers for its ability to stimulate the mind during the foul act of spellcasting. Even the repugnant darkstone is exploited. They chisel it using tools that seem arcane in nature, shaping it with rituals into a new form they call pure, yet clearly contaminated by magic.

When altered in such a way, this form of darkstone can be charged with lightning, stored in the very crystal, causing it to glow with disturbing and shifting hues. They are not ashamed to bring the power of the sky below the ground. Such accumulators, as they call the charged crystals, power rudimentary cannons, drills and many other deadly devices, large and small. The Vermin even prefer them to black powder, which they limit to small arms since they cannot handle large amounts properly.

Vermin use skewed mills to produce their "domesticated" lightning, which they then harness and transport along copper cables. When released in small bottles, the lightning serves to illuminate their caves. Not that they have much to be proud to show. But it allows them to see it in the deepest darkness, without gas lamps or runelight.

Vermin combine and transform all kinds of material. Hard or soft, liquid or gas, organic or mineral. An appalling liquid is used in their chariots and engines for fuel, an abomination unto the sanctity and solidity of the very mountains. They capture the toxic gas from deep chasms in tanks.

They use their canny noses and disturbed creativity to attempt insane combinations. Their recipes involve calcination, dissolution, separation, conjunction, putrefaction, sublimation and fermentation. They create unstable liquids and gases, kept in sealed canisters. When the seal is triggered or broken, the contents may explode, ignite, reek, suffocate, smoke, or even provoke strange biological responses: convulsions, tears, involuntary laughter. My skin was marked more than once before I learned to keep a safe distance. Itching can be severe. Sometimes even they seem surprised by the effects of their potions.

Vermin approach mechanics backwards. They use their tail like a long finger, exploring mazes of pipes. They show distaste for robust devices and love excessive complexity, perhaps because their slim fingers and long nails are adapted to fast and agile work. They dislike steam, which is too hot for them, and their seals can rarely resist the pressure. But they have developed a liquid which burns on contact with water. Whatever they achieve is randomly effective and predictably fragile.

Throughout my bondage, I was under permanent surveillance. Finally, I managed to "adjust" a particularly rickety experiment. It killed the scientists and a couple of guards. I clambered out of the rubble, bloodied and bruised. I was lost in their huge, filthy and illogical maze. I dug myself a tunnel out.

I have made my report. I will not speak of these things again. I will now resume my duty.

—From the records of the Guild of Metalsmiths, archives of Nevaz Barim

NOTABLE VERMIN

My eyes in the shadows show me many things. Ever faithful to your word, I provide this list as you requested for yourself and your fellow servants of the Dusk. It contains many of the most influential individuals in the city today, recommended as prime candidates for observation.

Frudjit the Gutter. The current leader of House Sicarra harbours bold and naked ambition. Low-born and known for brutal disembowelments, the Gutter has of late developed his own gut to an impressive size, growing large and round off the wealth of his clandestine activities. With senators and jent leaders in his pocket, and obviously favoured by the Free Rats he does business with, he has expanded his territory and his more or less illicit enterprises to new heights, even making deals with unlikely outsiders, from Makhar nomads to saurian enclaves. With operations now flourishing across many nearby colonies, I fear he will draw the eyes of the surface.

Status: Of interest.

Chivrit Khropchek. I'm sure the Dusk Senate's attention is already firmly drawn by this one. Born as Tiberius Haruspex to the prestigious and magisterial *jent* Opula, he chose a new name as a sign of plebian solidarity, declaring himself a full-fledged Gratchist and shaving the fur from his entire body (his retinue follows this fashion too). Seemingly a true idealist, Khropchek has been using his family's wealth to champion the downtrodden, and has won considerable success in electing tribunes favourable to his cause. Known for eloquent and bombastic speeches from the Senate floor, he is, like all populists before him, an inevitable source of trouble.

Status: Awaiting instructions.

Pontifex Sacrifa. Priests are well appointed to rile up the mob, but their purpose is to channel that fractious energy into safe, theological channels, not sermonise on the conduct of the Senate and House leaders – as a certain Sacrifa Juliana has begun. She is the leader of a relatively minor temple of Nameus, and a rare example of a female priestess ascended to the rank of Pontifex. But plague cult encroachments have made Nameus' shrines increasingly popular recently, and now the Pontifex parades around the city atop a vast Sacred Platform, blocking the streets with her throngs of followers, calling ever-more to her cause with the tolling of her remarkable iron bell, which has been adorned with favanite and anti-establishment augury. Every day, the great procession winds closer to the palace.

Status: Countermeasures prepared.

"Prof. Mauss". I was unable to find definitive information on this elusive individual – likely a pseudonym for one or more agents of House Rakachit known for the infiltration of human institutions and the invention of particularly potent weaponry. Their latest "rifle" would more aptly be called a cannon. If left unchecked, their talents could sway the balance of power in the city, or usher in the "technocracy" of which many Rakachit leaders have dreamed.

Status: Active pursuit.

Legate Septimus. Julius Septimus Rodentius Destrianus Claudius, to give his full name, has recently returned to the city after a victorious campaign against the dwarven holds of Taphria Minor. He can be recognised by his famous darkstone sword, and missing eye. A bloodfur legate beloved by his troops (and able to inspire exceptional discipline) is always a dangerous proposition, but one hailing from a powerful patrician *jent* supported by several important priests and Houses (including many of the Whiskers) is another thing altogether. Contributions from House Skorchit in particular have enabled much of his military success. The recent riots near the palace were provoked by the short-sighted consuls when they refused to grant Septimus a triumph. Additionally, it is said that he has already dispatched half a dozen would-be assassins personally, and double that number of enemy champions in battle.

Status: Immediate concern.

Jonch Krofij. Senator Krofij is well known to the mob. Throughout a long career, she has succeeded in making few enemies and yet acquiring extravagant wealth – a rare combination indeed. Yet of late I am worried by her growing ties to House Fetthis. Krofij sponsors major arena events with alarming frequency, and while she "humbly" refuses the spotlight, yet somehow the mob always knows that it was she who provided their beloved entertainment. I even have reason to believe that she has provided her fleshmasters the means to create more terrible monsters than ever before, no doubt on condition that she retains exclusive control.

Status: Infiltration initiated.

The Abyssal Claw. A Deeplord of House Stygia, this unnamed individual is said to cover his eyes with a steel hood to prevent him from ever glimpsing any source of light. While he has not yet made any moves towards the city proper, his great following among Stygians and many city Temples, to which he flagrantly "donates" rare gems, is a reason for concern. His behaviour has proven unpredictable – not long ago, his drills helped to drive off a bestial assault at Pityus, yet he has also attacked surface populations who posed no danger, without any consular authorisation. He may simply be an erratic warlord, but in my darker moments I worry that he could also be an agent of the rumoured cabal said to serve the Ratking. I know you do not believe such myths, but I would nevertheless advise enhanced observation in this case.

Status: Investigation required.

Joshua of Karsis. Said to have been baptised by a disciple of Barbas himself, the blind prophet Joshua of Karsis has proven a particularly militant crusader in the name of the heathen god Errahman. His pestilent zealots have abandoned the more peaceful techniques of the Plague Cult in favour of forced conversions across several colonies in Khasibbia. His adherents have already reached the city, stirring up conflict not just with the established temples, but also within their own cult. The Praetorians have curtailed their actions for now, but if Joshua himself ever chooses to come here, I dread to think of the destabilisation it could cause.

Status: Recommended for military action.

Kanrit Mustia. It seems it was not enough to exile this worrisome politician by naming her Proconsul of Provincia Æquitania, with a mandate to reclaim imperial colonies from the human barbarians who collaborate with supernals to soak that land in magic. Instead, she has coopted this same magic for her own purposes, surrounding herself with mage-priest supporters and even learning the arcane arts herself. Her propaganda paints her as the reincarnation of the female oracle-inventor Sycorax who became a dictator and conqueror of the Sixth Age. Reports suggest she is now actively conspiring from the burrow-fortress of Castra Nova to revolt against the Senate and declare independence, surely with herself as queen. This would set a dangerous precedent to others, especially the Council of the ever-riotous city of Galba Maior. If she does, in fact, plot to follow Sycroax into dictatorship, the threat would be immensely greater.

Status: Elimination underway.

The Shadowslice Stalker. Perhaps you were not expecting to see a member of your own Dusk Senate on this list. You may have your own opinion of this individual, but from the city streets I can report that her legend only grows. The plebs believe her to be a monstrous creature of dark magic, commanding the very shadows, able to turn herself to smoke and appear within the most secure burrow. My own observations depict a carefully curated legend, claiming credit for many of the most remarkable assassinations in our history. The Shadowslice mantle appears to be passed down over the years to preserve the mythos of an immortal and undefeatable foe. My concern is that such a careful attention to image belies an ultimate goal of personal power, unbefitting of a Dusk Senator. I would not, of course, voice such a concern to anyone who I did not trust most intimately.

Status: To be determined.

—Report discovered by operatives of General Fontaine and translated by vermin informants

THE RATKING

IT'S HERE... IT'S HERE. BENEATH US, AROUND US, EVERY ALLEY, EVERY PAIR OF BEADY EYES... I STILL HEAR IT, HEAR IT WHEN I SLEEP, HEAR IT WHEN I CLOSE MY EYES. IT KNOWS WHAT I WANT, WHO I AM - IT KNOWS!

THEY DIDN'T BELIEVE ME. I KNOW THEY DIDN'T, A CITY UNDER A CITY [indecipherable text] BUT I WASN'T MAD. NOT THEN. MOTHERS TELL CHILDREN "THE RATS WILL COME". MEN TELL JOKES IN THE TAVERN, BUT WE CHECK THE CORNERS FOR WHISKERS BEFORE WE LAUGH. I EXPLORED THE DARK PLACES, THE ONES WE ARE AFRAID TO THINK ABOUT.

THOUGHT I WAS CLEVER, WALKING ON SOFT FEET, ONLY A PATTER. DIDN'T HEAR THE QUIETER TREAD, TOO LATE, DOWN WE GO. MOST WOULD HAVE GOT THE KNIFE. KNIFE WAS THE KINDER CHOICE. I FOUND ITS AGENTS INSTEAD. THE CABAL WITHIN THE CABAL. HIDDEN EVEN FROM ITS OWN SWARM. BAG ON HEAD, WALKED FOR MILES. ACHED AND DIZZY. ON MY KNEES AND LIGHT AT LAST...

ONLY, THIS ISN'T REAL. STILL A DREAM. NOT A TRUE THING, BEG YOU. ONLY A NIGHTMARE CAN THIS BE, PLEASE. FLESH ON FLESH. BIG RATS, LITTLE RATS, ALL TIED BY TAILS, WRITHING. SCREECHING VOICES, MANY, DOZENS... ONE. ONE VOICE. ONE MIND. ONE TERRIBLE, AWFUL MIND.

I HEARD IT. I STILL HEAR IT. WE DID NOT SPEAK. COULD NOT SPEAK. NO LANGUAGE CARRIES SUCH GHASTLY TRUTH. I WAS A LOCKED DOOR. IT WAS A RAM, SPLINTERING ME. I HAD NO SECRETS, NO CORNERS. IT TOOK ALL IT WANTED FROM MY HEAD. A CHILD COULD FIGHT A GIANT WITH MORE SUCCESS.

THEN IT SENT ME OUT. LIKE A PUPPET ON STRINGS. LIKE SO MANY BEFORE. IT WANTED SOMETHING SMALL FROM ME. JUST A CELLAR TRAPDOOR LEFT OPEN IN THE UNIVERSITY. NO ONE NEED KNOW. SO SMALL A THING COULD NOT HURT.

I WAS NOT ALONE. GUARDS SLEPT. TORCHES UNLIT. ROOMS UNLOCKED. ALL TOGETHER, A TANGLE OF STRINGS - ONLY ONE MIND COULD PULL THE RIGHT ONES. AND DANGEROUS MAGICS ARE GONE. BUT I AM DISGRACED. I AM BLAMED. BECAUSE I SPEAK WORDS, BAD WORDS, TRUE WORDS.

I SAW IT TOO. SAW MORE OF IT THAN I CAN REMEMBER. I THINK ON IT AND MY MIND SCREAMS. IT EXISTS. HAS EX-ISTED, SINCE THE FIRST ARRIVAL. WILL EXIST. WITH THEM IT CAME, AND THEY SERVE IT. SOME DO, MANY DO, MOST WITHOUT KNOWING. EVEN SOME OF US ABOVE. IT WEAVES A WEB, AND WE ARE CAUGHT IN IT.

EVEN MOST RATS DON'T KNOW IT'S REAL. BUT US, THE INITIATED... WE ARE ITS TENDRILS IN THE SWARM. IT DRIVES THEM ON. FOR GLORY. A MAD CONSUMMATION. A WORLD-SWARM. IT MUST SURVIVE TO SEE. BUT ALL OTHERS CAN BE BURNED ON THE PATH. NO PIECE TOO IMPORTANT FOR SACRIFICE. LIKE A PLAYER OF GAMES, IT THINKS YEARS AHEAD. A THOUSAND PLANS FAIL, BUT WHEN ONE WORKS...THEN WE SUFFER.

RATKING IT NAMED ITSELF. MORTAL KINGS OF RATS ALL DEAD, BUT RATKING WILL NEVER DIE. NO... NO NO NO NO. NO MORE RATS. TAILS TIED, WRITHING FLESH. TAKE THEIR CROWNS AND GIVE ME PEACE. I STILL HEAR IT TALKING, WHISPERING TO RETURN. ONE MORE DARK DEED AWAITS. I MUST NOT... MUST NEVER...

—Ragged notes recovered from the philosopher Kapaneus'
cell in an Avrasi asylum after his escape in 843 A.S.

THE IX AGE
FANTASY BATTLES

Gather close, ye who would learn of the strange peoples and wondrous places of the Ninth Age. None of us can know the secrets of the entire world, but if you seek a little wisdom on a particular culture or nation, open up this tome and discover what there is to tell.

Perhaps you have glimpsed bright eyes in the dark, or heard squeaking in the night? You are right to fear, for the Vermin are much more than you imagine. In secret they have regathered their strength, and they intend to reclaim the mantle of a great and terrible empire.

Compatible with
IX
AGE
TM
The 9th Age™

www.ingramcontent.com/pod-product-compliance
Lightning Source LLC
LaVergne TN
LVHW080516200726
843507LV00008B/1116